Writer: Brian Augustyn
Illustrator: Jason Armstrong Colorist: Dan Waters

Dalmatian Press, LLC, 2003. All rights reserved. Printed in the U.S.A.
The DALMATIAN PRESS name and logo are trademarks of Dalmatian Press, LLC, Franklin, Tennessee 37067.
No part of this book may be reproduced or copied in any form without written permission from the copyright owner.

04 05 06 07 LBM 10 9 8 7 6 5 4 3 2
12547 JUSTICE LEAGUE: Total Eclipso

It was a bright spring afternoon in busy Central City. As always, the great city was host to many visitors. Some came to see the National Space Museum, where the history of humanity's reach for the stars was told in unique and exciting displays.

But the strange man in purple had not come to learn this history. Rather, he had come to claim a rare and powerful prize – a prize he planned to steal!

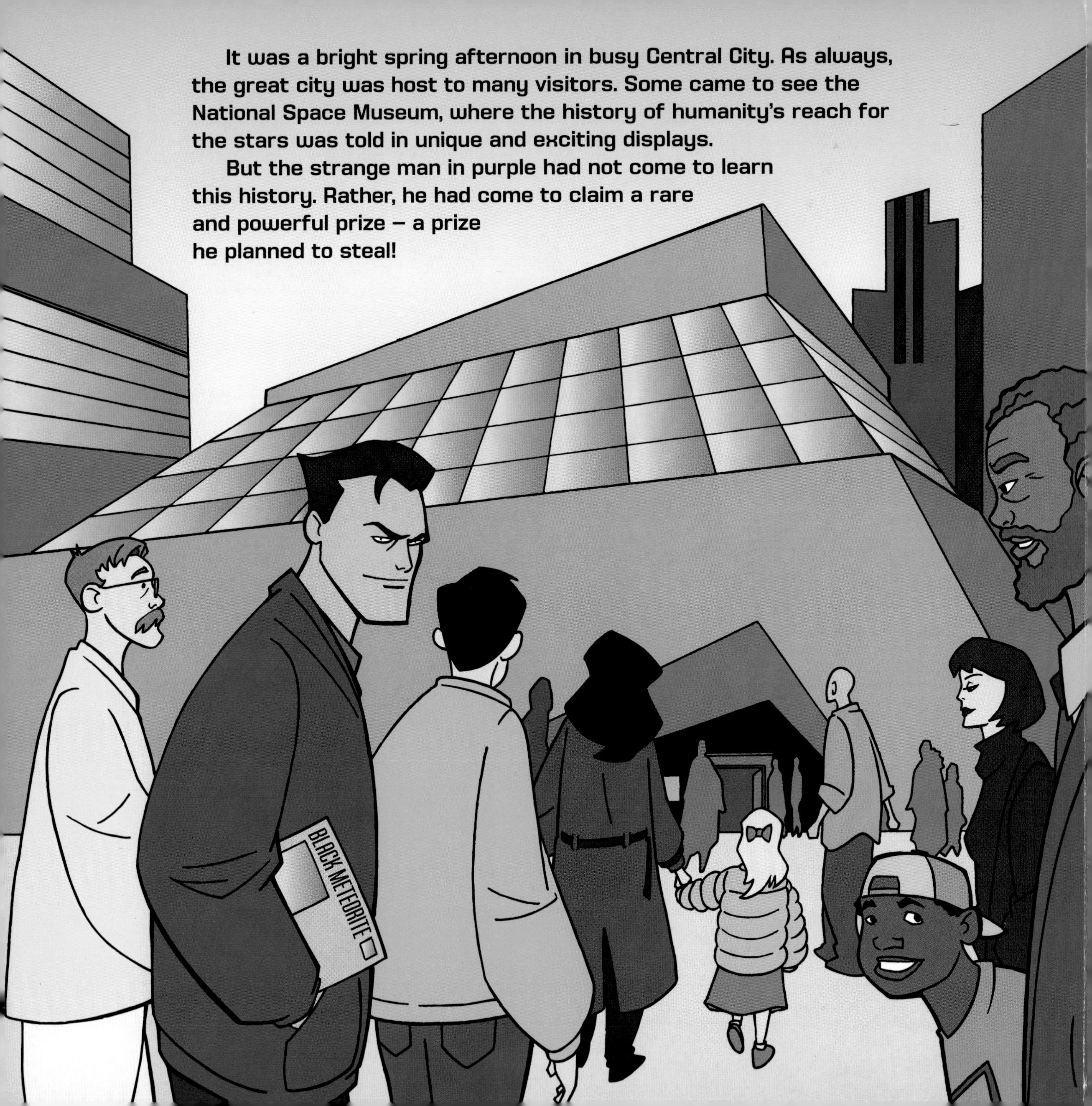
BLACK METEORITE

Weeks before, the gleaming black meteorite had crashed in the Nevada desert. Its origins were unknown, but the stone was fascinating to look at. Like a large dark jewel with light dancing off its many facets, it seemed to be alive, drawing all eyes with its mysterious beauty.

The strange man in purple was no ordinary man. He was under the control of the alien energy known as Eclipso, who lurked hidden within him. Now, with the man's hands on the treasure from the stars, Eclipso's evil energy was revealed to the terrified tourists.

"Stay back!" snarled the split-faced Eclipso as he grabbed the black stone. "This brilliant bauble is mine – along with all its cosmic power!"

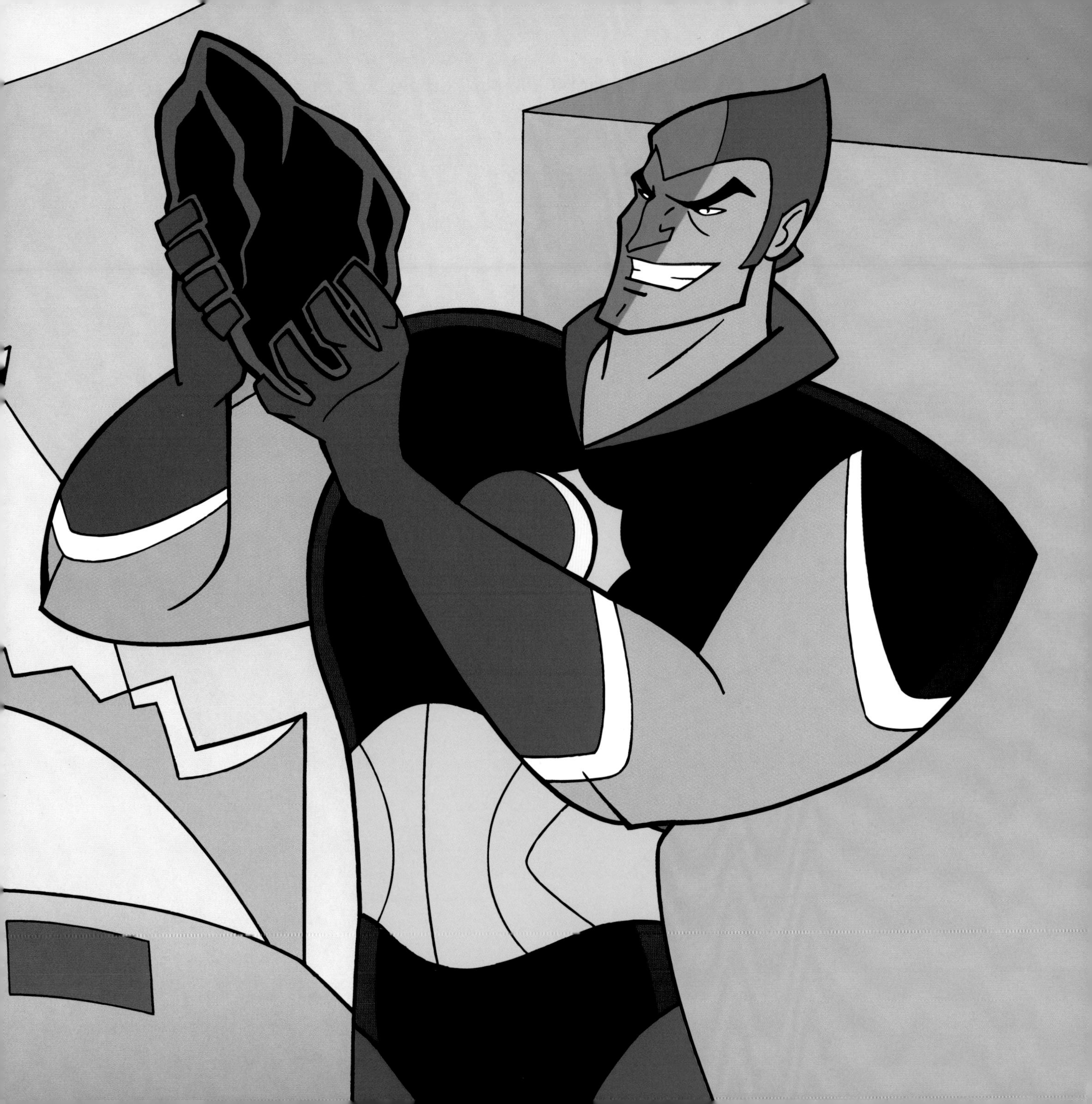

In the villain's hands, the meteorite blazed with an eerie violet fire. It was charged with incredible alien energy — energy that could destroy everything! The guards knew they were helpless against the villain.

"Call the police," someone cried. "Alert the Justice League!"

"Yes," Eclipso laughed with glee. "Bring on the Justice League! They will not defeat me again!"

Almost as quickly
as the call went out,
the world's greatest
heroes arrived on the scene! Wonder Woman,
Green Lantern, Hawkgirl, Martian Manhunter
and the Flash came to face their strange
alien foe once again.

"Remember, there are innocent
bystanders in there," warned Wonder
Woman. "Their safety is our
highest priority!"

"Let's make quick work of this split-faced creep!"
said Flash.

"Hopefully, we will do just that," said Green Lantern.
"But we don't know how powerful that weird meteorite is."

"Eclipso seems to think it's powerful enough to stop us,"
said Hawkgirl.

"Be alert and ready for anything,"
whispered Wonder Woman.

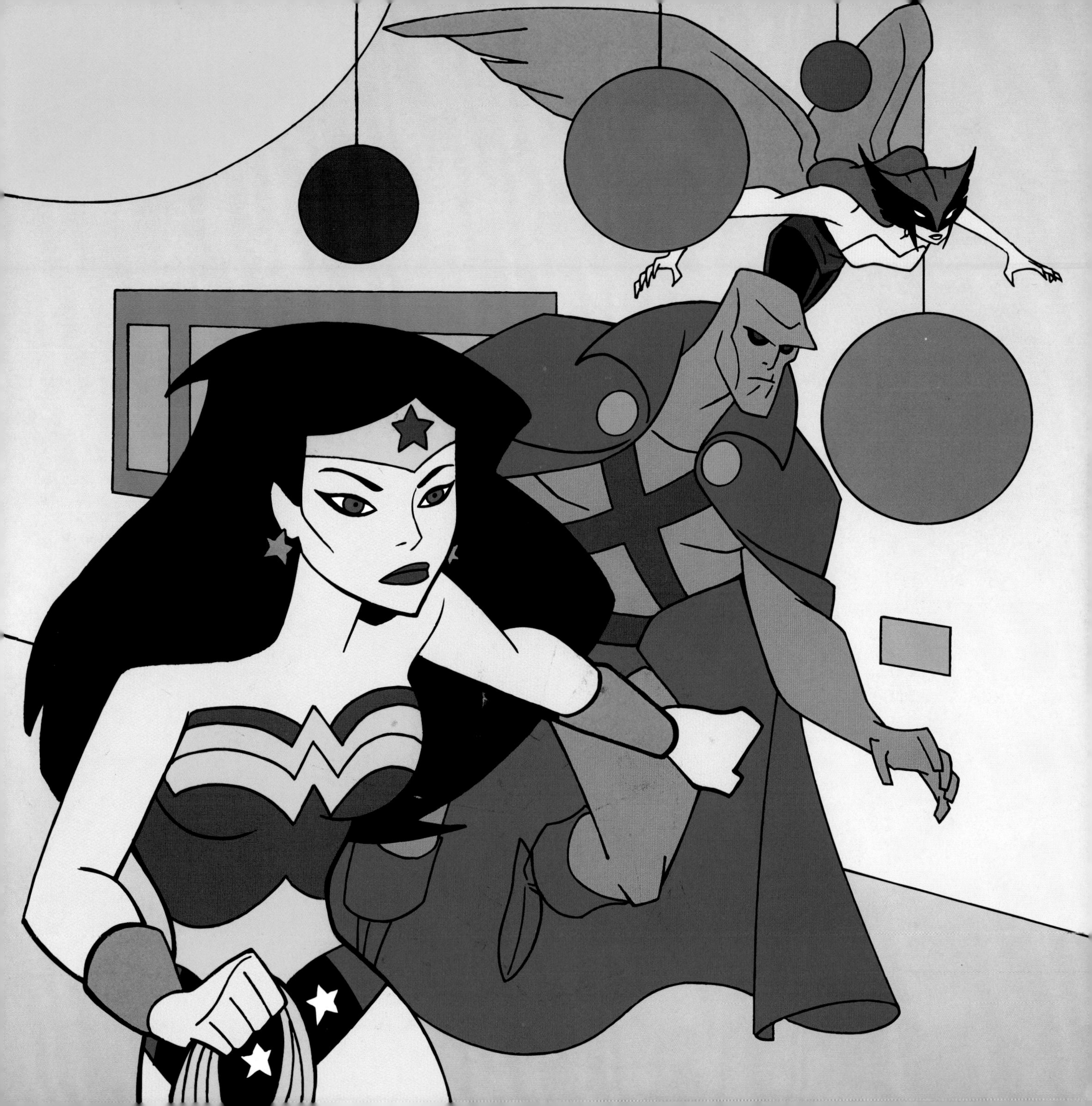

"I'd say Eclipso knows exactly what he can do with that rock," said Flash. "That's not good news for us!"

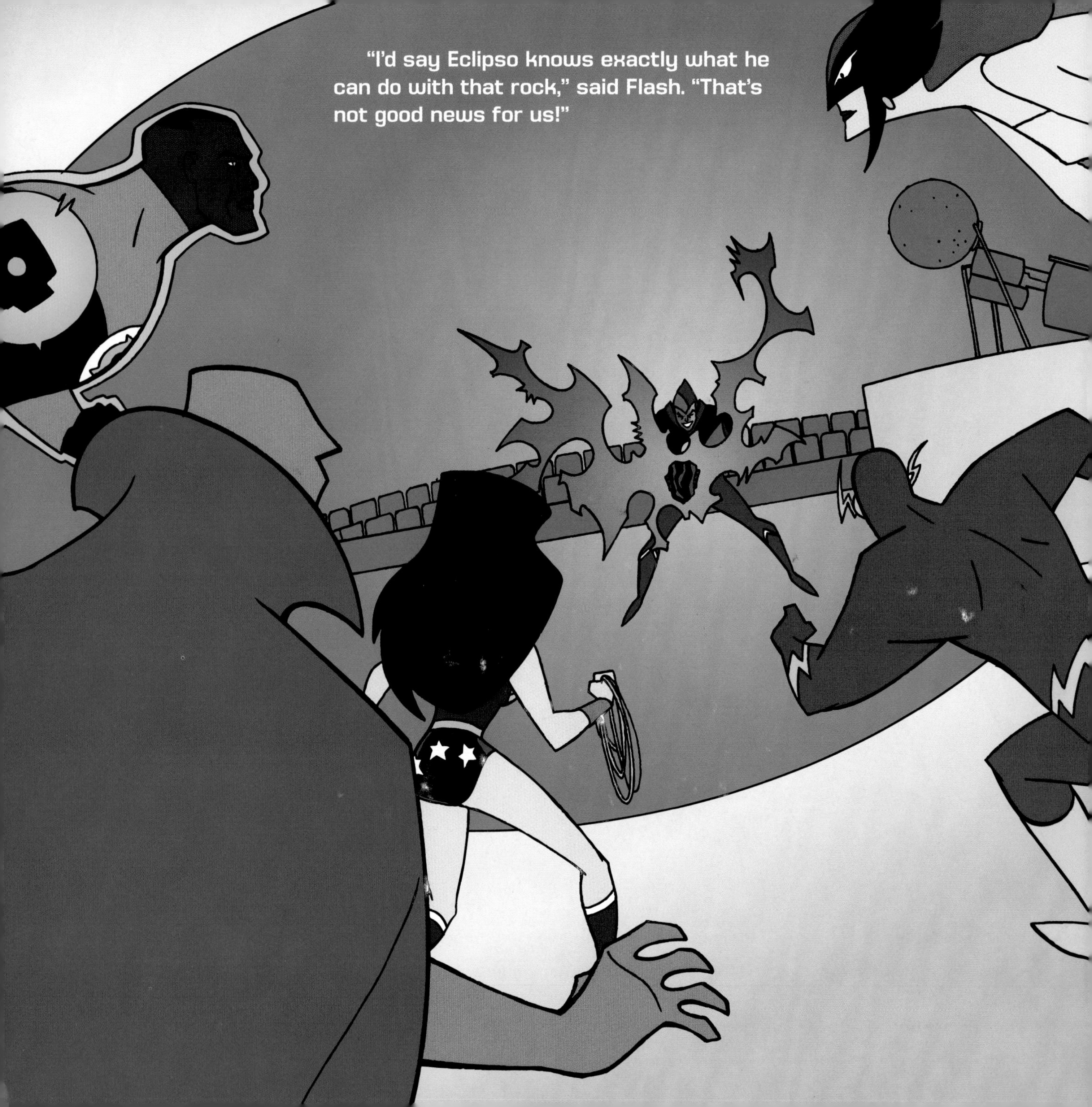

A sudden, blazing explosion took the heroes by surprise. Eclipso's new plaything was incredibly dangerous!

"This stone comes from the same dark corner of the universe as I do," cackled Eclipso. "It is packed with enough wild energy to destroy the Justice League... and, combined with my power, to pulverize this puny planet!"

Wonder Woman's amazing Amazonian lasso was itself a powerful weapon. Anyone caught in its coils was made to obey the Amazon Princess and speak the truth. If only she could lasso Eclipso...!

"I won't be caught like a rodeo bull, Amazon," sneered Eclipso. "Your shiny string is useless against me!"

Eclipso dodged through a door to another part of the museum. Clearly, the double-faced bad guy was making a game of his battle with the super heroes.

"In the past," he shouted, "you've always defeated me! This time, it's my turn!"

In the Moon Surface room, the heroes tried to maneuver over the cratered floor. They knew that one small step for them could be their last.

Eclipso picked up the heavy full-size lunar landing-craft model
as if it were a toy and hurled it at the defenders.
"Too much space history to handle, heroes?" laughed Eclipso.

Thanks to their mighty superpowers, and one giant leap by Martian Manhunter, the heroes escaped harm. But Eclipso had already scampered away, further into the museum.

Fighting fire with fire, Green Lantern unleashed the blazing emerald energy of his power ring.

Eclipso fought back with his own powerful energy. Waves of violet radiation battered the super heroes like wild hurricane winds.

"I will not be beaten again!" snarled Eclipso. "And I will have my revenge for every humiliation I've suffered at your hands!"

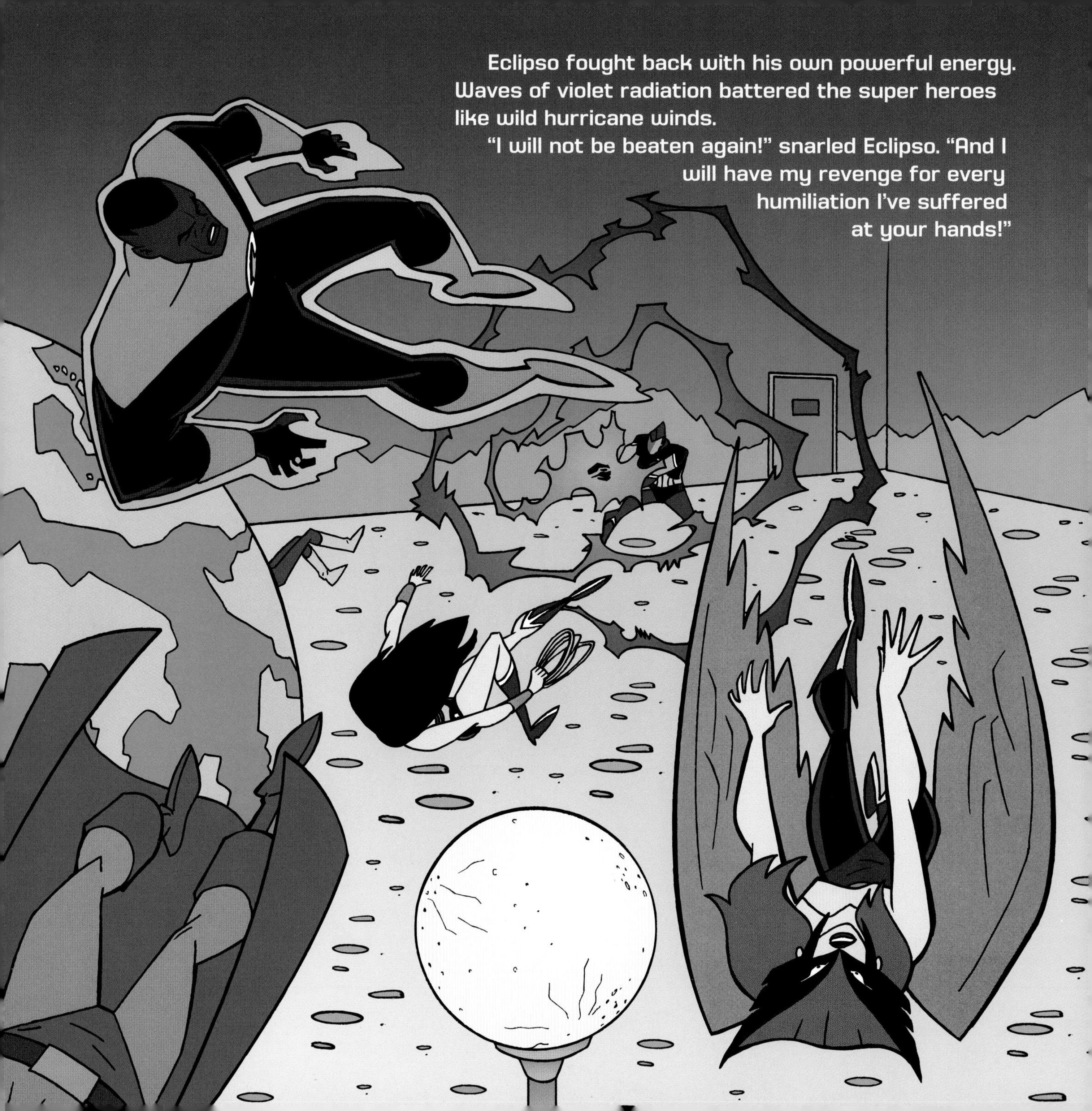

With all her Amazonian strength, Wonder Woman
launched a moon model at her foe.
Little did he know, Eclipso was about to be... eclipsed!

Slammed by the round model, Eclipso bounced violently away like a runaway billiard ball.

"Lunatic in the side pocket," chuckled the fleet-footed Flash.

Eclipso found himself in a sun-bright room, completely lined with magnifying mirrors.

"What... what are you up to, Justice Leaguers? It's so bright in here," said a waning Eclipso. "What is happening to me?"

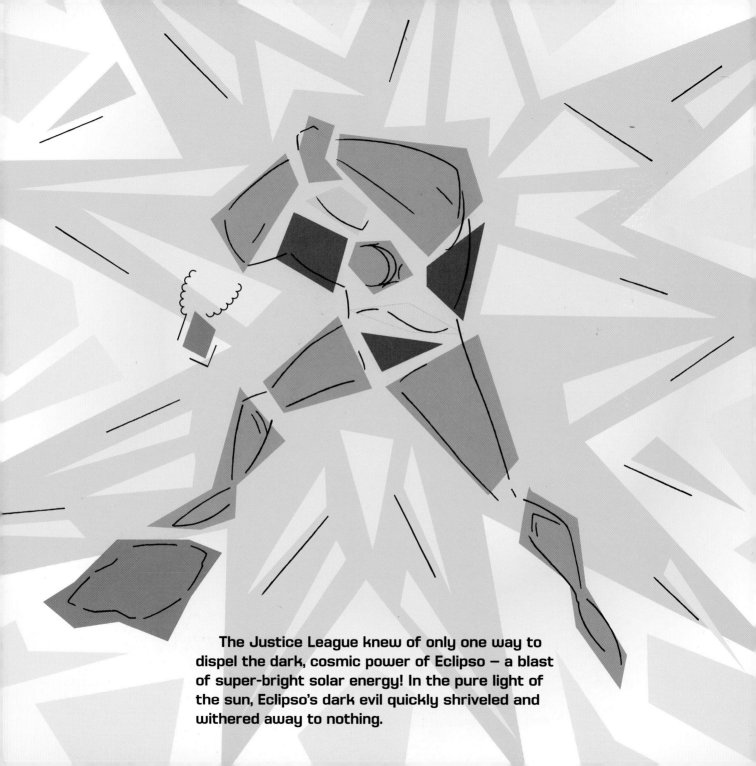

The Justice League knew of only one way to dispel the dark, cosmic power of Eclipso — a blast of super-bright solar energy! In the pure light of the sun, Eclipso's dark evil quickly shriveled and withered away to nothing.

With all of Eclipso's energy recaptured in a small, dark diamond, the heroes led the confused and innocent man in purple from the museum. He remembered nothing after picking up a black, sparking gem — never knowing that he had reached for a black diamond that carried Eclipso's power like a virus.

Now that the threat was over, the Justice League took charge of the meteorite and Eclipso's diamond.

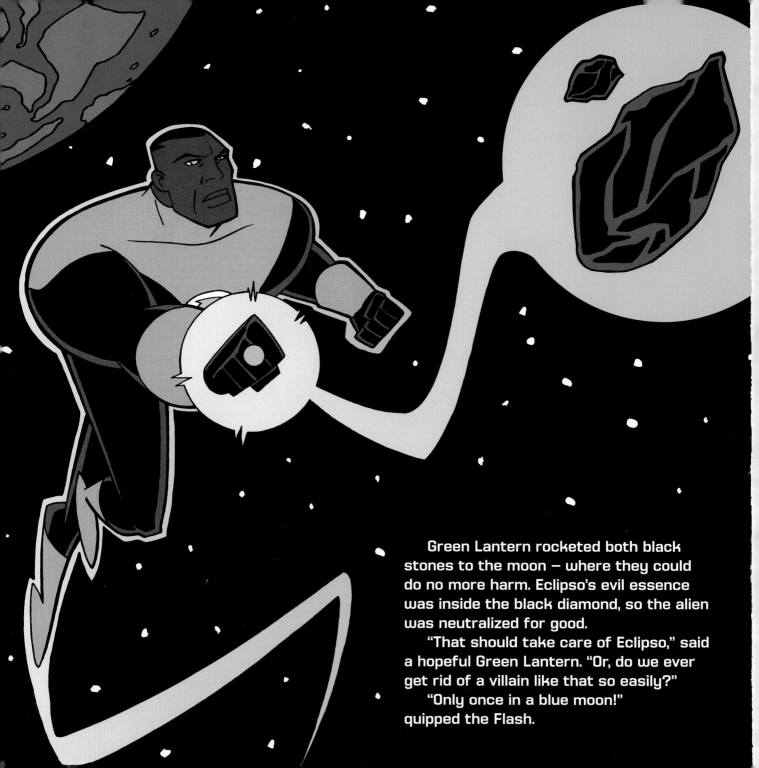

Green Lantern rocketed both black stones to the moon — where they could do no more harm. Eclipso's evil essence was inside the black diamond, so the alien was neutralized for good.

"That should take care of Eclipso," said a hopeful Green Lantern. "Or, do we ever get rid of a villain like that so easily?"

"Only once in a blue moon!" quipped the Flash.